GLITTER

CRAYON

To:

From:

WISH
LIST
-Sled
-Books
-Solar System
*Bike!

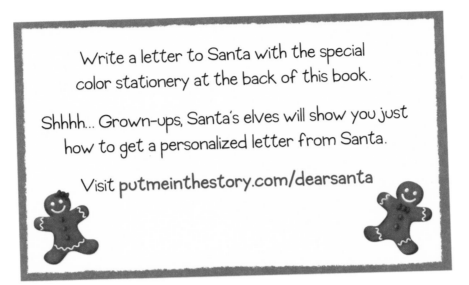

Write a letter to Santa with the special color stationery at the back of this book.

Shhhh... Grown-ups, Santa's elves will show you just how to get a personalized letter from Santa.

Visit putmeinthestory.com/dearsanta

For everyone who keeps trying to be the best they can be. –SLH

For my boys. Naughty or nice, I love you. –JJ

Copyright © 2019 by Sourcebooks
Text by Susanna Leonard Hill
Illustrations by John Joseph
Cover and internal design © 2019 by Sourcebooks

Sourcebooks and the colophon are registered trademarks of Sourcebooks, Inc.

The illustrations in this book were created digitally using Adobe Photoshop.

Published by Sourcebooks Wonderland, an imprint of Sourcebooks Kids
P.O. Box 4410, Naperville, Illinois 60567–4410
(630) 961-3900
sourcebookskids.com

Library of Congress Cataloging-in-Publication Data is on file with the publisher.

Source of Production: 1010 Printing Asia Limited, North Point, Hong Kong, China
Date of Production: July 2019
Run Number: 5015268

Printed and bound in China.
OGP 10 9 8 7 6 5 4 3 2 1

Dear Santa

words by Susanna Leonard Hill

pictures by John Joseph

sourcebooks
wonderland

Two weeks before Christmas, Parker's weekend art class buzzed with excitement.

Ms. Holly clapped her hands for attention.

"Boys and girls," she announced, "it's time to write our letters to Santa! Don't forget to draw him pictures of what you'd like for Christmas!"

Parker's friends got right to work.
They talked about how good they'd been...

Dear Santa,
    I always help Mommy with the groceries...

Dear Santa,
    Last year I was good, but this year I was SUPER good!

Dear Santa,
Grandma says I am a
perfect little angel...

Parker was a little surprised to hear this.
Everyone made mistakes sometimes, but his classmates
made themselves sound perfect.
Parker knew he was *not* perfect.

Parker also knew a thing or two about Santa.

Santa knew when kids were bad or good. It said so right in the song, for goodness sake.

There was no use pretending you'd been good if Santa already knew otherwise.

Nope. It was best to be honest…but it might mean… NO PRESENTS!

With a sigh, Parker began his letter.

Dear Santa,

Let me explain...

I tried to be good. Really.
But sometimes, it is VERY hard!
For example, Brussels sprouts. YUCK!
They smell bad and taste worse!
But I will try to do better.

About July, when I didn't brush my teeth for eleven days, here's why:

I had two loose teeth and I didn't want them to fall out.

Mom and Dad said they'd grow back.
But what if they didn't?

What if everyone else's teeth grew back, but I had a giant space where I could never bite pizza again?

I'm sure you can understand how risky brushing was!

They fell out anyway, and I hope you know I've been brushing carefully ever since, because two new teeth came in!

When I stayed up past bedtime three nights in a row, it was because I was making Mom's birthday card and it was a secret!

I'm sorry for breaking the bedtime rule, and for all the glue and glitter, and for Mom having to wash everything a lot of times to get it out.

But I think she liked the card...

Anyway, I guess I haven't been that good. It's not easy being a kid. There are so many rules! But I'm doing the best I can. So here's my Christmas list in case you think it's still okay to bring me something.

A bike

A Super Slider Sled 3000

New books

A glow-in-the-dark solar system for my ceiling

Your friend,
Parker

Parker gave his letter to Ms. Holly.

The next morning, when handing out a special Christmas decoration assignment for the class, Ms. Holly added a special note for Parker about his letter to Santa: *I'm sure Santa will appreciate your honesty and willingness to be responsible for your actions. I know I do. Merry Christmas.*

The next day, Ms. Holly sent the letters to the North Pole…

Santa got so much mail, he had a whole room just to keep it in. He read letter after letter after letter about how well behaved and wonderful everybody was.

And then he got to Parker's letter…

When Parker woke Christmas morning, he couldn't help hoping there would be at least one present for him.

He peeked into the living room and whooped with joy when he saw the presents under the tree! With his name on them!

On top was a letter.

Dear Parker,

Your letter made me smile. Let me explain...

It was nice to get a letter from someone who knew he made mistakes sometimes and was willing to admit it and take responsibility. Your letter was honest and kindhearted. For every "naughty" thing you may have done, you did many more good things for your friends and family. Nobody's perfect, but perfection is not required—just keep being the best version of you that you can be.

Have a very merry Christmas, and keep up the good work!

Your friend,

Santa

PS: I'm not wild about Brussels sprouts either.

Now it's your turn to write a letter to Santa!
Get an adult's help cutting out these pages.